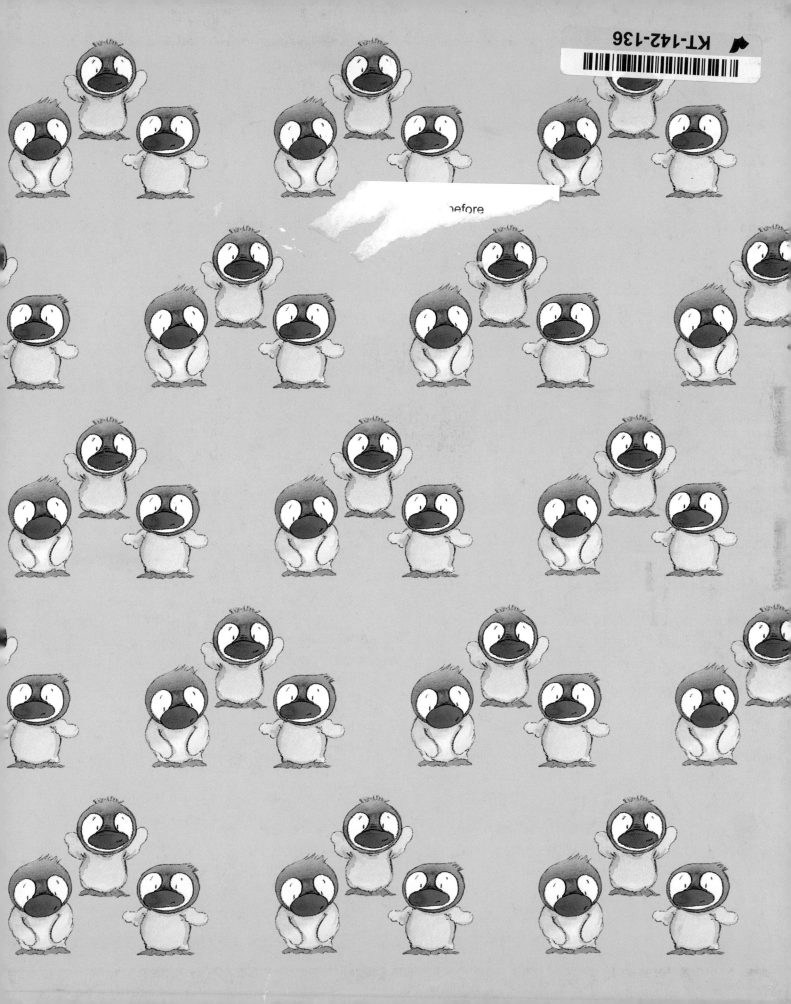

before

First published in Great Britain in 2001 by Brimax
an imprint of Octopus Publishing Group Ltd
2-4 Heron Quays, London E14 4JP
© Octopus Publishing Group Ltd

ISBN 1 8585 4203 0
Printed in Italy

Can't, Shan't, Won't!

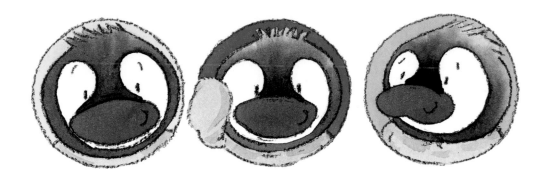

In a land of ice and snow,
where the wild wind blows, live three very
naughty penguins. They are called
Can't, Shan't and Won't.
Whenever Mother Penguin asks the little
rascals to help her, they shuffle
and slither away as fast as they
can on their slippery,
flippery feet, and
pretend not to hear her.

Today Mother Penguin wants the little
penguins to catch some fish for supper.
As soon as they hear her calling,
"Can't... Shan't... Won't!"
the naughty penguins race down the slippery
slide and hide in an ice cave.
But Mother Penguin is pretty good at sliding
too, and very good at finding ice caves,
so she soon catches them out.

"Now!" gasps Mother Penguin,
shaking the snow from her flipper-like
wings and panting for breath.
"I need your help. You must catch
some big, fat, juicy fish for supper."
The three little penguins
look up at her sadly.

"Can't," says Can't.
"My flippers are too cold."
"Shan't!" says Shan't. "My feet are too cold."
"Won't!" says Won't. "My beak is too cold."
"Nonsense!" says Mother Penguin.
"You are penguins. You like the cold!
Now here are your fishing rods -
off you go."

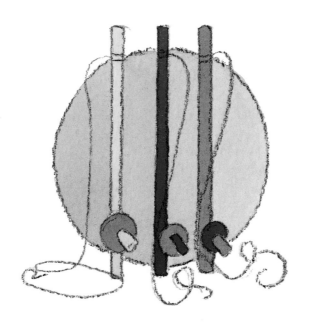

So the three little penguins slide
off across the snow. Icy Lake is always
frozen over, but every now and then there
are little round holes which the seals use
to come up for air. These holes are perfect
for patient penguins to catch fish from.
But Can't, Shan't and Won't are not
patient. They cannot sit still
for a minute.

"I can't see the point in sitting here,"
says Can't, after just one minute,
peering into the hole.
"I shan't be able to catch a thing," says
Shan't after just two minutes.
"My line is tangled up."
"I won't ever be warm again," says Won't,
after just three minutes, and
shivering from his beak to his feet.
"Let's go home!"
shout Can't, Shan't and Won't.
So they set off across the ice,
without a single fish.

"Can't go home without fish, Mother will
be cross," says Can't, slipping on the ice.
"Shan't have anything for supper!"
says Shan't, sliding down an icy bank.
"Won't go home again,"
says Won't, skating on one foot.
So they decide to run away!

The little penguins skip and scamper all the
way to where the icy land meets the sea.
There they jump onto an iceberg, and before
very long, the iceberg slides away,
floating along on the waves.

The little penguins are very scared.
What's your name" asks an old walrus.
"Can't!" cries Can't. "Can't ever stop!"
"What's your name?" asks a snowy seal.
"Shan't!" sobs Shan't.
"Shan't ever get home!"
"What's your name?" booms a huge whale.
"Won't!" weeps Won't.
"Won't ever run away again!"

Still the iceberg sails on. Soon it
is dark, and the moon rises over the
snow-capped sea. It is very cold, and
by now the penguins are very very scared!
Then suddenly the wild wind begins to blow.
It blows the iceberg in a circle.
It blows the iceberg across the waves.
It blows the iceberg back to shore,
where the icy land meets the sea.
And there, waiting for the
little penguins, is Mother.

"Thank goodness you're safe!"
She hugs each little penguin in turn.
"We were lost!" cries Can't.
"We were cold!" sobs Shan't.
"And we haven't any fish!" weeps Won't.
"Never mind," says Mother Penguin.
"Father has caught plenty, so we can have
a nice fish supper. Let's go home."
Off they ride on Father's sledge, back to
their warm, safe house in the snow.

After supper Mother tucks the penguins
into their warm cosy bed.
"I can't believe we were so silly," sighs Can't.
"I can," laughs Mother Penguin.
"We shan't run away again,"
mumbles Shan't.
"Home is the best place to be,"
agrees Mother.
"And we won't ever be naughty again!"
yawns Won't, with just a hint of a twinkle
in his one open eye.
"We'll see!" smiles Mother Penguin.
"Sweet dreams, Can't, Shan't, Won't".

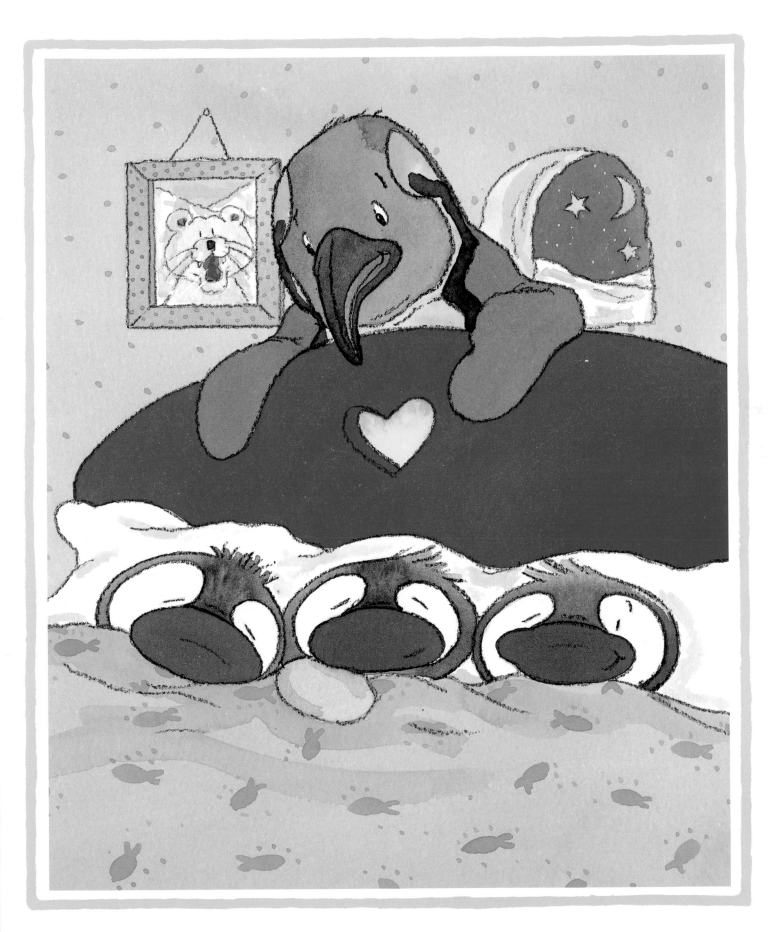